Gabby God's
Little Angel ™

This book belongs to:

"Kate" Love Aunt Dawn

my God Daughter You

GOD

BLESS YOU

GABBY, GOD'S LITTLE ANGEL™

© 2011 by Sheila Walsh

Illustrations by Marina Fedotova

Published in Nashville, Tennessee, by Tommy Nelson®. Tommy Nelson is a registered trademark of Thomas Nelson, Inc.

Published in association with the literary agency of Alive Communications, Inc., 7680 Goddard Street, Suite 200, Colorado Springs, CO 80920. www.alivecommunications.com

Thomas Nelson, Inc., titles may be purchased in bulk for educational, business, fund-raising, or sales promotional use. For information, please e-mail SpecialMarkets@ThomasNelson.com.

Unless otherwise noted, Scripture quotations are from the International Children's Bible®. © 1986, 1988, 1999 by Thomas Nelson, Inc. All rights reserved.

Page design by Mark L. Mabry

Library of Congress Cataloging-in-Publication Data

Walsh, Sheila, 1956-
  Gabby, God's little angel : sent to show God's love / Sheila Walsh ; illustrated by Marina Fedotova.
     p. cm.
  Summary: Assigned to protect a young girl, guardian angel-in-training Gabby realizes her new assignment will be a bigger challenge than she expected.
  ISBN 978-1-4003-1715-8 (hardcover)
  [1. Guardian angels--Fiction. 2. Angels--Fiction.] I. Fedotova, Marina, ill. II. Title.
  PZ7.W16894Gab 2011
  [E]--dc23   2011022115

Printed in Mexico

11 12 13 14 15 RRD 5 4 3 2 1

Mfr: R.R. Donnelley / Reynosa, Mexico / August 2011 / PPO 123743

Gabby God's Little Angel™

Sent to Show God's Love

By Sheila Walsh

Illustrated by Marina Fedotova

Tommy
NELSON®

A Division of Thomas Nelson Publishers

NASHVILLE   DALLAS   MEXICO CITY   RIO DE JANEIRO

ngels, angels, line up. Well done, everyone. Hmmm . . . has anyone seen Gabby?"

"She fell over her harp, sir," Parker said. "I think she took it to have it . . . well . . . straightened out."

"And she is in guardian angel training!"

Raffles the senior angel replied, shaking his head.

"I think she's funny!"

said Raoul, Gabby's best friend.

"And she talks a lot . . .

I like that!"

"I'm here! I'm here!"

Gabby said. "Sorry I'm late, sir. I had a . . . well, how shall I say it? It was a . . . no, not really, it was more of a, well, and yet . . . on the other hand . . . you could describe it as . . . oh dear, perhaps just a musical mishap!"

"Welcome, Gabby. Glad to see you survived your . . . mishap," Raffles said with a grin as the other angels giggled.

"Today, you receive your new assignments!" Raffles began.

"One of the most important jobs God assigns to angels is to protect those He loves. Take a look."

The angels peered excitedly over the edge of the cloud. "That . . . is a playground," Raffles said, pointing to the children playing below.

"They're playing with the ground . . . really?" Gabby said. "Wow, that doesn't seem like it would be a ton of fun, but I guess I don't know as I've never really had a 'ground' or played on it or with it or under it."

"Look at the girl climbing the tree,"

Gabby said.

"That doesn't look very safe, but it does look really fun, like woo-hoo fun!"

"That's Sophie," Raffles replied. "She needs a *lot* of protection."

"She may need a very big, ginormous angel," Gabby said.

"Well, Gabby," Raffles replied, "the Lord has chosen YOU for this big job. You seem to have a lot in common with Sophie!"

Just then, Gabby tripped and was dangling upside down from the rainbow.

"Woo-hoo, Sophie," Gabby cried. "Woo-hoo for me and you!"

"I am so-o-o excited!"

Sophie told her friend Missy after school that day. "So excited that bursting is quite a possibility. In fact, I would put it in the 'quite probable' category!"

"What are you *so-o-o* excited about today, Sophie?" Missy asked with a grin.

"My pony!"

Sophie replied. "I get to ride my pony, Glitter, for the very first time. For days I have only walked her round and round in circles until we are both dizzy, but now . . . today . . . ta-da . . . I get to ride her!"

"Be careful, Sophie,"

Missy said. "Remember what happened with that pony last summer."

Sophie laughed, remembering how she was facing the wrong end of the pony when she finally managed to get in the saddle.

"Well, it WAS nice to see where I had been!"

Sophie said with a grin.

That afternoon, Gabby followed Sophie and her mom to the stable. It is one of God's mysteries that neither of them could see or hear Gabby.

"Oh my, you are a big, big, big, big pony!"

Gabby said.

"Now listen here, horsey, Sophie is precious cargo. Do you understand?"

The pony shook her head and whinnied as if she understood.

"The Lord loves her very, very much. So no funny business!

Not a waddle to the right or a toddle to the left."

"Are you ready, Sophie?" her mom asked.

"I am definitely ready!" Sophie replied. "My readiness is about to take wings and fly!"

"Okay, okay," Mom said with a laugh.

"Just be careful!"

"Why, I think I could be a professional pony rider!" Sophie bragged as she slowly rode Glitter around the corral.

"I think we could be ready for the Olympics by next week!"

Just then, a dog ran into the corral and started barking.

The noise scared Glitter, and she began to buck.

Gabby was surprised, too, and went spinning through the air.

"Help!" Sophie cried as she tried to hold on to Glitter's reins. "Help me! I'm about to launch into outer space!"

Gabby rushed to keep Sophie from falling off Glitter.

"Don't worry . . . I've got you! I'm here, it's all good, no panic, we are under control, oops not so much . . . okay, now I've got you!" Gabby shouted, but of course, Sophie couldn't hear what she was saying.

Just as Gabby got to one side of Sophie, the little girl began to
slip off the other side of the pony.

Gabby quickly cartwheeled over Glitter
to keep Sophie from slipping off.

As Glitter finally came to a halt, both Sophie and
Gabby took a deep breath.

"Wow . . . that was a wild ride!"

Sophie said.
"Phew . . . this job is going to be harder than
I thought!" Gabby said with a sigh.

At bedtime, Sophie admitted, "That was just a little, tiny bit scary today when Glitter started bucking. But I almost felt as if someone were protecting me."

"Someone was," her mom said. "Do you know that God loves you so much and has

promised to send His angels to watch over you?

That's how precious you are to Him."

"Like a *real* angel? Like a flying-with-wings angel?" Sophie asked. "But I didn't see anyone."

"Here, let me read this Bible verse to
you, Sophie," her mom said.

"'He has put his angels in charge of you.
They will watch over you wherever you go.'

That's God's promise to you, Sophie."

Sophie knew exactly what she wanted to pray about
that night.

"Dear God, thank You so much for sending
Your angel to help me stay on my pony today.
I'll try not to be so much trouble tomorrow.

I'm so glad You love me. Amen."

Back in heaven, Gabby looked down to make sure
Sophie was sleeping peacefully.

"How is your new assignment going, Gabby?" Raffles asked.

"Today wasn't easy. No sir, not at all," Gabby said.

"Sophie is going to keep me VERY busy indeed.

I'll be flying to the right,

I'll be swooping to the left.

I'll be zooming back and forth.

I'll be . . . I'll be doing all I can to show Sophie just how much

God loves her!"

The Lord is your protection. . . . He has put his angels in charge of you. They will watch over you wherever you go.

–Psalm 91:9, 11